The Little Book of
BEDTIME STORIES

www.alligatorbooks.co.uk

The Alligator logo is a registered
trade mark of Alligator Books Ltd.

Published by Alligator Books Ltd
Gadd House, Arcadia Avenue
London N3 2JU

Printed in India

Contents

Daisy's First Adventure

On Sunday mornings when Sam and Sara went to the park, Sara always took her doll Daisy along with her.

Now, although Daisy didn't want to be left at home, she did find her trips to the park rather boring.

While Sam and Sara played ball Daisy was left lying in the grass looking up at the sky, and when they played hide-and-seek or climbed trees, Daisy was left alone propped up in the corner of a hard park bench.

"I wish I could go round the park instead of staying in one place all the time," the doll thought to herself… and on this Sunday morning Daisy was about to get her wish!

There were times when Sara's brother, Sam, could be quite a naughty boy, and as they ran across the park, he snatched Sara's doll and hurled her high into the air.

"Something exciting is happening to me at last!" gasped Daisy as she flew over the trees. Down below she could see children sailing toy boats on the lake, people were cycling and skating and jogging round the park, and everybody was having so much fun.

All of a sudden, Daisy was lifted up in the fluttering tails of
a passing kite. A strong gust of wind took her all the way round
the park, and as she looked down, she saw Sam and Sara searching
for her in the long grass by the trees. The next moment the wind
dropped, the kite fluttered and dived down towards the lake. But
just before it hit the water, Daisy let go of the kite tails and jumped
onto the deck of a toy sailing boat.

"That was lucky," Daisy giggled to herself as she sped across the
water. It was her first trip on a boat, and it was wonderful.

As the sailing boat reached the edge of the lake an inquisitive duck swam across. Perhaps he thought Daisy was a slice of bread or a piece of tasty duckweed, for he grabbed her in his beak and hurried towards the shore.

But when he discovered that Daisy was no good to eat, he waddled out of the pond and dropped her in the long grass by the trees.

"Look! There's Daisy!" yelled Sam looking very relieved. "She must have been here all the time!"

"Promise you'll never, ever throw Daisy away again," said Sara holding onto her doll tightly.

Sam promised he wouldn't, but Daisy hoped he would. This was her first big adventure and she longed to have another one just as exciting!

Lawrence Goes Adventuring

On days when Lawrence woke up and remembered there was no school, he went ADVENTURING!

"I'm in the greenhouse today," he told his mum and dad.

"You're going ADVENTURING then!" they said smiling, and they opened the back door wide.

"Hat!" said Dad.

"Packed lunch!" said Mum. "Do try to be home for tea!"

Now it has to be said, greenhouses can be boring at times… but not this one!

Lawrence marched down the garden path to the greenhouse and flung open the door. In he strode, bold as could be…the noise was DEAFENING!

Squawking, squeaking, howls and hisses, growl, buzz, honk and ROAR!

"It's a jungle in here!" chattered a little monkey swinging down from a palm tree.

"Tell me about it!" replied Lawrence, failing to notice that a Giant Pincher Beetle had just landed on top of his hat.

"Time to cross the river," said Lawrence.

"Look out!" shrieked the monkey!

But Lawrence never saw the crocodile open its mouth wide, or heard its jaws close with a SNAP!

He was far too busy eating the egg and cress sandwiches his mum had packed for his lunch.

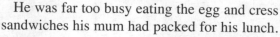

"Be careful, there's something hiding in the long grass!" warned the little monkey jumping up and down.

But Lawrence was enjoying his banana, and didn't even catch a glimpse of the tiger's sharp sparkling teeth.

"Don't move another step," whispered the little monkey quietly. "There's a giant snake sliding down from the tree."

But Lawrence didn't hear the snake hiss, he was trying to open his fizzy drink.

Then Lawrence sat down on the steamy jungle floor and took out his last slice of cake.

"Ah, an elephant!" he cried. "Can you take me home in time for tea?"

"He's back!" called Mum when she saw Lawrence fling open the greenhouse door.

"How was your adventuring?" Dad asked eagerly.

"Very quiet today," Lawrence replied, and went inside for his tea.

Tina and Twink, the Mermaid Twins

Tina and Twink were mermaid twins whose home was a beautiful coral reef, like a garden under the sea.

All kinds of creatures lived in the warm clear water around the reef. Every one of them loved the two little mermaids and went to visit them each day…this morning was no different…

First, a shoal of shimmering rainbow fish came by and wanted to play. Tina and Twink chased them and raced them all through the coral caves, until they caught up with them on the other side.

Then the tiny rainbow fish gathered into the shape of a heart – just for the two little mermaids.

"That's wonderful, you clever things!" said Tina blowing them bubble-kisses.

"Off you go, all of you!" laughed Twink clapping her hands. "We've something very important to do today."

And with a flick of their tails, the mermaid twins darted through the water, scattering the tiny rainbow fish in all directions.

Now earlier that morning, Tina and Twink had promised their music teacher they would practise tunes on their trumpet shells.

"We had better get started before any more of our friends call round to visit," said Tina, and both of the mermaids took a deep breath, ready to blow into their shells.

But right at that very moment, two rather friendly young turtles stopped by.

"Come for a ride to Seaweed Wood and see how fast we can go!" they called out to the mermaids.

"Sounds like a great idea!" cried Tina putting down her trumpet shell.

"It's better than practising tunes all morning," giggled Twink.

And with a flip and a flick of their mermaid tails, the mischievous pair leapt onto the turtles' backs and took off.

Both turtles whizzed through the water at tremendous speed, curving and swerving in and out of the swaying seaweed.

14

Very soon they completely forgot that the mermaids were riding on their backs, and they nearly flipped over a number of times.

"That was amazing!" gasped Tina and Twink when the turtles came to stop.

"Now we must go home and practise on our trumpet shells as we promised," said the little mermaids.

"But neither of the turtles could remember the way back!

"I'm afraid we're lost, and it's all our fault," said the poor turtles looking rather sorry for themselves.

"Don't feel bad," said Tina kindly.
"It's our fault too, we should have stayed at home
and practised."

"Let's play our tunes right now," suggested Twink, and she
picked up one of the trumpet shells that lay on the seabed and
began to play.

"It might make us feel better," sighed Tina, and she joined in
with the music.

The two little mermaids played every tune they knew over and
over again, and the turtles listened quietly.

All of a sudden they saw a bright shimmering flash, and the
shoal of rainbow fish came darting out of the seaweed.

16

"Are you still practising your tunes?" asked the fishes altogether. "It's getting rather late. Time you two went home!"

With frisking tails and flips and bounds, the tiny fish gathered themselves into the shape of an arrow, and led everyone back to the coral reef.

"We kept our promise after all," said Tina when they were tucked up in their shells that night.

"I'm so glad we did," replied Twink drowsily. And the two little mermaids drifted off into a deep asleep.

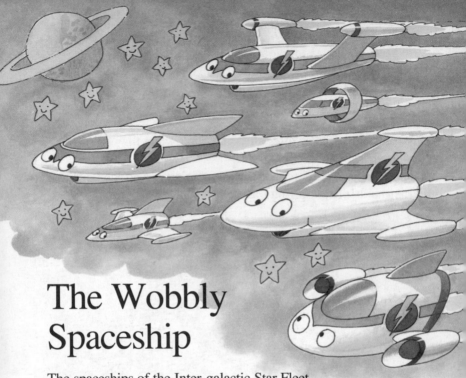

The Wobbly
Spaceship

The spaceships of the Inter-galactic Star Fleet
were ready at all times to be sent on vital missions across the galaxy.

As soon as the alarm sounded at their Control Base, they set off
at hyper-speed through space.

For problems on planets, colliding shooting stars, runaway
rockets or any astro-disaster, the spaceships of the Inter-galactic
Star Fleet were always on hand.

But one spaceship was different from the rest!

At first he was sent on missions with the rest of the fleet, but it
wasn't long before the other spaceships started to make fun of him.

"Wibble! Wobble!" taunted one .

"You're just like a jelly!" jeered another.

All this teasing made the poor spaceship feel very ashamed, because it was true…he did wobble!

For however hard he tried, he could not stay upright for long. First he flew to the right, then tilted to the left, and more often than not, he would overbalance and start to spin.

He was indeed, a very wobbly spaceship!

And if that wasn't bad enough, he found it impossible to land… which is bound to happen if you wobble.

If ever he did manage to reach a planet, he would bounce across the surface like a pebble skimming over water. In a way that was lucky, because the wobbly spaceship always managed to avoid large rocks and missed falling into deep craters.

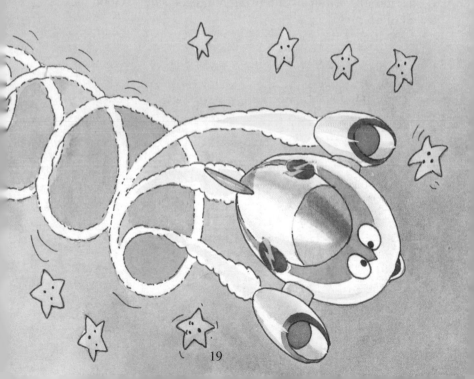

Other travellers in space got out of the way the moment they saw him flying unsteadily towards them.

"If my flying doesn't improve," said the spaceship sadly, "I'll be thrown out of the Inter-galactic Star Fleet!"

Then one day he was close to the Control Base when the alarm sounded. "Emergency! Emergency! A manned rocket has been reported missing for over a week. All spaceships return to base immediately!"

Swiftly the whole Inter-galactic Fleet assembled to hear their instructions.

"This is your most important mission so far," they heard the voice of their Base Controller say. "Search everywhere for the missing astronaut and bring him back safely. Good luck all of you!"

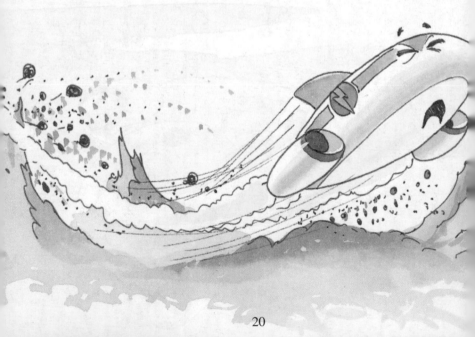

As the fleet of spaceships set off, one of them shouted to another.

"Wibble! Wobble! The Jelly will save him!" and the rest of them sniggered as they whizzed by.

Feeling very hurt, the wobbly spaceship set off a bit behind the others, for it was quite clear that they didn't want him around.

He searched the galaxy for hours and hours. Sometimes he flew to the right, then he tilted to the left, but all the time he kept a sharp lookout for the missing astronaut.

After flying for so long, the wobbly spaceship needed a rest and tried to land on a nearby planet. He bounced across the surface – as he always did – then he bumped into something hard and metal, but luckily came to a stop without a single scratch.

"You're here at last!" he heard a voice call, and standing there was the missing astronaut.

"My rocket ran out of fuel and crashed here over a week ago. Am I pleased to see you!"

And with that, the astronaut jumped aboard the wibbly wobbly spaceship, took off from the planet and steered towards home.

The spaceship had never flown so fast or so straight before. He didn't tilt to left or right and he couldn't overbalance if he tried.

It felt just wonderful!

"All you needed was a pilot," laughed the astronaut. "Now all I need is a spaceship like you!"

…and from then on, the two of them conquered space together.

Sadie Keeps a Secret

Every year when summer came around Sadie and her best friend, Phoebe, would go camping.

On the morning of their holiday it always took ages to pack everything they needed into Sadie's little car.

The boot was so full of luggage they could hardly close the lid. Also squeezed into the back seat were a couple of skateboards, Phoebe and Sadie's large tent, and a smaller one for Sadie's dog, Tippi.

The girls couldn't go on holiday and leave Tippi behind, could they?

Now best friends should always tell each other their secrets, don't you agree?

But this year Sadie had a secret she wanted to keep from Phoebe…
just for a little while.

"I must be taking a lot more clothes than
last year," said Phoebe looking at all her
extra cases.

"Me too," said Sadie bringing out more
and more bags.

"We'll never get all this stuff in the car," Phoebe sighed. "I'll have to leave some of my clothes behind."

"No you won't," laughed Sadie as she fetched a huge sun umbrella and two tennis racquets.

"We're not leaving Tippi's new puppy behind, are we?" asked Phoebe with dismay.

"Don't worry," smiled Sadie. "They'll be plenty of room for her."

Phoebe shook her head. "There's no way everything will fit into your car," she said looking at the growing pile. Then she gave a little shriek. "We've forgotten the tents!"

"No need for tents any more," said Sadie mysteriously. "Look what's parked in front of the garage!"

Right next to Sadie's little car was a brand new camper van.

"Do you like the colour?" Sadie asked her best friend.

"I love it," gasped Phoebe. "How did you manage to keep it secret?"

"It was really hard," Sadie laughed. "Now let's pack the van and go on holiday!"

Farmer Barley's New Friends

Farmer Barley was busy in his fields all through the year, there was plenty of work to be done. He got up very early every morning and was always late to bed at night.

Most days Farmer Barley jumped in his tractor and drove off into the fields, but he never had anyone to talk to, except a lot of crows and a friendly-looking scarecrow.

At the start of the year Farmer Barley would plough the soil ready for setting seeds in the spring. And in summer, when the corn needed cutting, he would climb up into his massive combine harvester and work until darkness fell, with only the owls to keep him company.

Although Farmer Barley enjoyed working on his large farm, he sometimes felt lonely. Then one day, the farmer's wife came into the yard with a wonderful surprise for him.

It was a sheepdog!

"Thank you, my dear," said Farmer Barley. "I shall call her Meg. Now we must have some sheep for her to round up."

So the farmer bought some sheep.

"How about a cow or two for me to look after?" the farmer's wife asked – she could get lonely too when the farmer was away in the fields all day.

So he went off to market and bought some cows.

"Little pigs would be nice!" Farmer Barley said as soon as he got home.

"Let's buy a goat," added the farmer's wife, "and don't forget a few hens!"

"Our farm will be even busier now," laughed Farmer Barley.

"And we'll never feel lonely again." said the farmer's wife.

I think she wanted lots of animals all along, don't you?

Princess Goldie and Geraldine

If you believe in wishes and enchanted fountains, then this story is for you...

Although Princess Goldie lived in a magnificent palace with countless servants, she often felt lonely. Her loving parents, the King and Queen, gave her everything she asked for, but what Princess Goldie wanted most of all was a friend.

Every day she would go outside into the palace gardens and play all alone by the fountain.

"I'll pretend this fountain is enchanted and make a wish," said the Princess out loud. So she closed hereyes tightly and, as you may have guessed...she wished for a friend. Surprise, surprise, when the Princess opened her eyes, waddling across the lawn was a large white goose.

"At last, I have a friend!" cried Princess Goldie, and she ran towards the goose and gave her a great big hug. "I shall call you Geraldine, and we'll do everything together!"

And so they did.

Geraldine went to live with the Princess in the palace. The King and Queen were delighted and didn't mind a bit, and soon the goose became part of the royal family – they even had breakfast together.

The Queen fed Geraldine dainty slices of buttered toast, and the King gave her half his cereal that popped and crackled. Princess Goldie's favourite breakfast was a blueberry muffin, and now she shared it with her goose every morning.

The magnificent royal palace was full of empty rooms and endless corridors, can you think of a more perfect place to play?

For the very first time, the King and Queen heard whoops of joy from the Princess as she chased Geraldine all round the palace.

Sometimes the goose would chase the Queen, which made the King laugh until tears rolled down his cheeks, and he had to beg Geraldine to stop.

Princess Goldie's days were never dull again, for the goose made sure she had plenty of fun.

"I wish I could dance!" exclaimed the Princess one day. To her surprise Geraldine knew all the new steps, and showed her how they were done.

The King and Queen watched for a while then joined in. They hadn't danced for years, but they soon got the hang of it!

After breakfast one morning, when Princess Goldie and her goose had gone outside, the Queen said to the King, "We ought to give Geraldine a present, she has brought so much happiness to us all."

The King thought this was a wonderful idea and sent for the royal jeweller immediately.

The very next day, the royal couple presented Geraldine with a beautiful golden crown.

"For the best friend in the world!" Princess Goldie declared as she placed the crown on Geraldine's head.

Then one terrible morning, when Princess Goldie was late going outside after breakfast, she thought she saw Geraldine flying away.

"I must be mistaken," she cried racing across the lawn. The Princess called and called, but before very long the goose had flown from out of the palace grounds and disappeared beyond the trees.

"Perhaps it's not Geraldine," said the Queen trying her best to comfort her daughter.

"I will send every servant in the palace to look for her," the King promised when the goose hadn't returned by nightfall.

Where, oh where was Geraldine?

The weeks passed by, everyone searched high and low, but no trace of the goose could be found.

Poor Princess Goldie thought about Geraldine all the time. She couldn't sleep, and she didn't want to eat she was so unhappy.

"Our palace is awfully quiet," said the Queen, "you can almost hear a pin drop."

"No one dances any more now Geraldine has gone," the King sighed. "Soon I'll have forgotten all the steps."

And when the three of them sat down to breakfast each morning, nothing seemed the same. The Queen didn't want her dainty slices of buttered toast, and the King pushed away his bowl of cereal that popped and crackled.

Then one wonderful, magical morning everything changed!

When the princess saw her favourite blueberry muffin she had an idea. Quickly she grabbed the blueberry muffin off the plate, ran outside and stood by the fountain.

"I'll pretend this fountain is enchanted and make a wish," said the Princess out loud. So she closed her eyes tightly and, as you may have guessed…she wished that her goose would come back.

Surprise, surprise, when the Princess opened her eyes, Geraldine was busy pecking at the blueberry muffin…and right behind her were six golden goslings!

Princess Goldie was overjoyed, so were the King and Queen, and from that day on the palace was filled with noise and laughter once more…not to mention lots and lots of dancing!

Digby Clears the Road

Brad came running out of his office into the yard.

"I've just had a phone call, there's an urgent job for us!" he shouted to Digby, his yellow digger. "A pile of earth is blocking the main road into town. It needs moving right now!"

Digby was busy shifting sand into a waiting dumper truck.

"Last scoop then I'm finished!" called Digby.

Once the dumper truck was full, it was about to pull away when Brad shouted across to Digby again.

"I'll just be a minute. I need to find my hazard jacket and put it on, this job could be dangerous and I need to be seen clearly."

Now the dumper truck heard everything Brad said.

"This sounds exciting," he thought to himself. "I'll try to find out what's going on!"

When the dumper truck reached the site where the sand was needed, a cement mixer was parked nearby.

"A huge landslide has blocked the main road into town!" the dumper truck told the cement mixer excitedly.

"They've sent for Digby, shall we follow him?"

"Count me in!" said the cement mixer starting up his engine.

Straight away the dumper truck tipped his load of sand, then the two machines moved off together.

Coming down the road towards them was a bulldozer with its blade off the ground.

"Listen to this!" yelled the cement mixer. "The mountain has fallen across the main road into town!"

"Sounds like a big problem," said the bulldozer. "There's bound to be lots of stones and huge rocks, not to mention massive boulders!"

"They've sent for Digby and we're following him," said the dumper truck.

"Wait for me!" cried the bulldozer. He didn't want to be left behind and miss all the excitement.

"Where are you lot going?" enquired a road roller as the dumper truck, the cement mixer and the bulldozer passed by.

"The mountains have fallen, there is rubble everywhere, and the main road into town is completely blocked. They've sent for Digby and we're following him!" gasped all three of the machines together.

"Mind if I tag along?" asked the road roller. "I move rather slowly, but I get there in the end." And he rumbled off behind them. When they reached the blocked road, Digby was already moving earth and Brad was putting out cones.

"How about a bit of help?" said Digby with a grin…he was very pleased to see the four machines.

"There's a lot of earth to shift, and urgent repairs to be done before the road can be opened."

"That's why we followed you here," said the cement mixer.

"We were told that the whole mountain had fallen onto the road!" the road roller mumbled.

Brad looked puzzled. "Now where did you get that idea?"

The dumper truck kept quiet and so did the other machines.

Every one of them had added a bit to the story and made things sound worse than they really were.

"You're all here now, so let's get started!" shouted Digby.

Before very long a van full of workmen arrived to lend a hand, and after a lot of hard work all the earth was moved, the cement mixer repaired the edge of the road and the roller flattened the ground…the main road into town was opened at last.

"Well done!" said Brad to all the machines.

"We made quite a team, didn't we?" laughed Digby.

Mabel's Terrible
Temper Tantrums

Mabel astonished everybody with her terrible temper tantrums.
She had to have her own way all the time, and if not, she would
scream and scream and scream, and yell and bawl at the top of
her voice…it was deafening!

Worse still, if she was really cross, she would jump up and
down with temper, kick the furniture and slam the doors.
This made the whole house shake so much, the neighbours
thought it was an earthquake…and who can blame them?

Toys and books were thrown all over the room every time Mabel got mad, then the cat would dash under the table and the dog would follow double quick…it was scary to watch!

Mealtimes were a nightmare with Mabel at the table. She quite liked soup and small iced buns with cherries on top…but nothing else at all.
Did she eat her vegetables? Of course not!
Take cover, Mabel has been given a plateful of peas!

Then one day Mabel was taken to the zoo.

"I didn't want to come!" she screamed stomping past the penguins. "And I'm not going to look at any of the animals!" she yelled as she clomped past the chimps.

Perhaps an ice-cream might keep her quiet…and in a strange way it did.

Mabel took one lick and dropped it in front of the lion's cage…what a disaster!

She opened her mouth wide, took a deep breath – Mabel was about to have the most tremendous temper tantrum.

All of a sudden the lion moved to the front of his cage, he opened his mouth too, he took a deep breath, and gave an almighty ROAR!!!

The whole zoo trembled.

Very slowly, not making a sound, Mabel backed away and tiptoed past the lion's cage.

And from that day to this, she has never again had a temper tantrum.

In fact, she is the sweetest, gentlest, quietest little girl you could wish to know.

Eddie and Ted, Ghost Hunters

Late one night, by the light of the moon, Eddie and Ted went ghost hunting.

"Let's try over there," said Eddie pointing to Wailing Wood.

"This hollow tree looks spooky!" shouted Ted, and he banged on the trunk and stuck his head inside.

"Come out, ghosts, we know you're there!"

"I bet they'll come out when they see me," said Eddie, who had brought along his Monster Mask.

Impatiently the boys waited and watched, but all they saw were a few vampire bats and the odd giant spider hanging from the tree.

"There's nothing much here," grumbled Ted.

"Then I think I'll go home to bed," muttered Eddie.

"Hold on!" said Ted. "I thought I heard a groan."

"Be quiet and listen," whispered Eddie. "I'm sure I heard a moan."

"WE KNOW YOU'RE THERE!" both boys hollered.

"SO COME OUT NOW!"

Ted, who always had his Master Beam Torch when he went ghost hunting, shone it up into the tree. Low and behold, hiding in the branches were a whole family of ghosts.

"Go on, scare me silly!" ordered Ted.

"Please frighten me to death!" begged Eddie.

The ghosts looked embarrassed… one even turned red.

"Give us a few blood-curdling screams," pleaded Ted.

"Shriek, wail, screech…anything to scare us," begged Eddie.

The ghosts shrugged their shoulders and hung their heads.

"We don't know how to scare anyone," piped up the smallest one.

"You see, none of us have ever been taught how to scare properly," another ghost muttered. "I couldn't even frighten a mouse."

Eddie and Ted stared at the ghosts in disbelief.

"Your moans and groans sound like tummy rumbles!" and the two boys screamed with laughter.

The ghosts had to agree, and they all sighed quietly.

"What you need is A REALLY BIG SCARE!!!" yelled Eddie and Ted as loud as they could.

The ghosts clung to one another with fright.

"Meet us tomorrow," said Eddie and Ted mysteriously, "and we'll take you for a ride."

And so they did…in fact, the next day, the ghosts went on every ride, at Thunder Island theme park. Their shrieks, and wails and spinechilling screams were terrifying to hear. Eddie and Ted were very proud of them.

So now…never go near Wailing Wood after dark, the ghosts in there are far too scary!

The Monster
Behind the Fence

Francie loved her little dog Tasher,
and Tasher loved Francie. When
Francie was at home Tasher was
happy all day long, but when she
went off to school, Tasher was
miserable. He would howl loudly
as soon as she left the house. Then
Francie's mum would put Tasher
out into the garden so she could
have a bit of peace and quiet.

Not that Tasher kept quiet! He
would bark and yap, then yap
and bark until Francie came home
from school.

One morning, when Tasher had
stopped barking for a minute,
he discovered a hole in the garden
fence and wriggled underneath.

"I've never been in a wood before," thought Tasher as he scrambled out on the other side of the fence. The woods looked so interesting, he forgot all about barking and yapping for once, and scampered towards the trees.

"Hi there!" a little brown rabbit called to Tasher. "You're new round here, come with me and meet a few of my best friends."

"An excellent idea!" replied Tasher, and without so much as a bark or a yap, he followed the little brown rabbit into the wood.

A grey and white badger poked his nose out of a deep hole, and a fox cub peeped out from behind a tree, a hedgehog stopped by to see what was going on…each one had come to take a look at Tasher.

"It's so good to meet you all," said Tasher, who had always
wanted to have some friends. "Strange I've never seen any of
you before and I live close by."

"None of us go beyond the edge of the wood," whispered the
badger. "We're all too frightened."

Tasher's tail stopped wagging at once.

"A terrible fierce monster lives there behind a garden fence,"
the hedgehog explained.

"There's a hole underneath the fence, and if ever the monster
escapes, it will gobble up every single one of us!" the fox
cub added.

Tasher pricked up his ears.

"None of us have ever seen the monster," said the little brown rabbit," but we can hear the scary noises he makes all day long."

Tasher looked puzzled. "I've never seen this monster, and I live behind the fence."

When Tasher heard how worried his new friends were, he began to bark very loudly. "I'm going to find this terrible monster and chase him away for you!"
The little dog sounded so fierce.

In a flash, every one of Tasher's friends vanished, and he was left all alone.

Tasher stopped barking at once and looked round in surprise. Where had everyone gone?

After a while, to his delight, he saw the little brown rabbit hopping towards him with the others close behind.

"We've guessed who the monster is!" they shouted. "It's you!"

"Make that noise again!" cried the little brown rabbit eagerly.

"You mean barking," laughed Tasher, and he barked and barked until the sound echoed round the wood... and this time none of the animals ran away. Instead, one by one, they followed Tasher through the hole underneath the fence and scrambled into the garden.

When Francie got home from school that afternoon it seemed strangely quiet, Tasher wasn't barking as usual.

Straight away the little girl ran out into the garden, perhaps something was wrong. What if her little dog had run away?

Francie was astonished to find Tasher in the middle of the lawn with the animals from the wood. "You kept on barking because you felt lonely when I was at school," smiled Francie. "All you needed was a few friends!"

Will Anna Miss the Show?

Anna loved to dance. She went to classes two evenings a week and the whole of Saturday morning.

Like all of her classmates, Anna dreamed of becoming a ballerina.

Then one day Anna was given some very exciting news. Miss Sweetly, who taught her ballet class, had been asked to put on a show in a real theatre.

"You can all take part if you wish to," said Miss Sweetly smiling at the girls, "but we shall have to start practising right away."

Everybody in the class was thrilled and gathered round to be shown their new steps.

"I can see I'm going to be busy too," laughed the lady who played the piano for dancing.

Later when Anna returned home, she could hardly wait to tell her family.

"I'm going to dance in a beautiful costume on a real stage," she called as she flung open the front door.

Then, to her dismay, she tripped over a rug and fell and hurt her ankle…what a disaster!

Anna had to be taken to see the doctor without delay.

"You've bruised your ankle badly," he said. "There'll be no dancing for a week, but you will be fine in time for the show."

Anna was very upset to miss her dancing, but her mum promised to take her to Miss Sweetly's class, soshe could watch the others and learn the steps.

That night as Anna was going to bed, she had a very clever idea.

"If I take my ballerina doll with me, and move her arms and legs into the right dance positions, it will help me remember my steps for the show."

Anna's idea worked brilliantly. After a week her ankle was better and she went back to Miss Sweetly's class.

"I'm amazed," Miss Sweetly gasped as she watched Anna dance with the others. "You know the steps of every dance perfectly, well done!"

The theatre was packed on the night of the show. The girls looked beautiful in their new costumes and danced like real ballerinas. Miss Sweetly was so proud of them for giving such a splendid performance.

Anna had never felt so happy, and that night she gave her ballerina doll a special hug for all her help.

A Whale of a Tale

Crystal Cove Harbour was so busy the Harbour master sent for his nephew, Chad, to give him a hand.

"I've never seen so many boats coming in and out," said the Harbour Master. "Everybody wants my help, and I can't be in two places at once."

"Don't worry, Uncle," replied Chad cheerfully. "I'll soon sort things out."

"A fishing boat has just tied up at the jetty, there's a problem with the engine!" Chad's uncle called as he hurried to find out what was the matter.

"IT'S ON FIRE!!!" yelled Chad, and he grabbed a bucket, filled it with water from the harbour, then threw it onto the smoke and flames.

Luckily it put out the fire straight away.

"Thanks a million, you've saved my boat," said the fisherman shaking Chad by the hand. "If the fire had spread, it could have destroyed every boat in Crystal Cove Harbour."

Later that night, when all the boats had been safely tied up, Chad and his Uncle were walking along the jetty gazing out to sea.

"Look there, Uncle, a whale!" cried Chad pointing.

As his Uncle watched the whale spouting water, he came up with a clever idea.

"Crystal Cove Harbour needs a very special boat to do a very special job," he told Chad.

"I shall order one first thing in the morning."

Next day when the new boat arrived, it really was special.

"A FIREBOAT!" cried Chad as he jumped on board. "I know there isn't a fire, but can I try it?"

"Certainly!" laughed his uncle. All the boats that come into Crystal Cove Harbour will be safe from now on!"